GODZILLA ATE MY HOMEWORK

GODZILLA ATE MY HOMEWORK

BY MARCIA THORNTON JONES

ILLUSTRATED BY ROBERT KROGLE

A
LITTLE APPLE
PAPERBACK

SCHOLASTIC INC.
New York Toronto London Auckland Sydney

ISBN 0-590-37236-X

12 11 10 9 8 7 6 5 4 3 2 1   7 8 9/9 0 1 2/0
                                                40

Printed in the U.S.A.

First Scholastic printing, September 1997

To Steve Jones, thanks for your encouragement, help, and support!

CONTENTS

GODZILLA ATE MY HOMEWORK

1

THE PERFECT PET

"Pleeeease?" I drew it out as long as I could. I batted my eyelashes three times like I had to hold back big puddles of tears. Mom looked up from the stack of bills she was trying to pay.

"Parker," she said. "I've told you before, pets are too much trouble." She pointed to

1

the mound of papers on the kitchen table. "Now stop bothering me. I'm busy."

"But a guinea pig is the perfect pet," I told her. "It's small and cute and it will only eat a little bit. It would be no trouble at all!"

Margaret stomped into the kitchen. She always stomps because she is always mad at something. Margaret is my sister, but ever since she started middle school she pretends she doesn't know me.

"You are not letting Parker get a rat, are you?" Margaret asked. I made sure Mom wasn't looking and I stuck out my tongue. Then I smiled my most innocent smile when Mom looked back at me.

The phone rang and Margaret hopped across the floor like it was on fire. "I'll get it!" she shrieked, even though Mom and I didn't budge. Mom says all teenage girls are like that when the phone rings because they hope some cute boy is going to call them.

Margaret said hello. She giggled and her voice got all gooey. She tried to whisper, but Mom and I heard everything since we were about as far away from her as a frog could hop. I rolled my eyes and Mom smiled like she thought something was funny.

"A guinea pig is not a rat," I told Mom, trying to get her back on a topic more important than Margaret.

Mom sighed. "Remember what happened to your goldfish?" she asked.

I thought about Glip and Glop, my two giant goldfish. All they did was swim in circles, but they still made a mess. The water got cloudy. Green scum grew on the glass.

"I thought the soap would help make the water clean," I told her. "But I know better now. I'm older." I stood up tall and straight. I hoped Mom would notice how tall I had grown. "Mr. Morris says I am a very responsible second-grade boy." I thought it was a good idea to mention my teacher.

Mom looked like she was ready to cave in.

"Pleeeease?" I said again.

Margaret put her hand over the mouthpiece and shushed me. I lowered my voice to show Mom how good I could be.

"I'm the only kid in the second grade without a pet," I told Mom.

"You really can't expect me to believe that," Mom said.

I nodded so hard I got dizzy. I counted out names on my fingers. "Marcus has a pet lizard, David has a dog, Mary has three kittens, Tricia has a pet hamster . . ."

Margaret shushed me again and I stopped reciting all the second-graders' pets.

Tap. Tap. Tap. Mom's fingernail landed on the stack of bills. "Pets cost money," she said.

I was ready for this argument. It was what Mom always said when I wanted something. I dug deep in my jeans pocket and pulled out a crumpled wad of green bills. "I did just what you told me. I saved all my allowance for something I really want. I really want a guinea pig. I have enough money, too."

Mom looked at the crumpled money in

my hand. She sighed again. "Well," she said, "you'll have to ask your father."

I waited until I left the kitchen to do a little jump. The guinea pig was almost mine. After all, Mom was the tough guy in our house.

2
GODZILLA

Before I could get in the door of The Wagging Tail Pet Store, Dad put a hand on my shoulder. "Are you sure you want to do this, Parker?" he asked.

Sometimes my parents asked the silliest questions. "Of course," I told Dad. I tried not to sound like I thought he was the dumbest man on earth.

"A pet is a big responsibility," he said. "Remember the goldfish?"

I wished everyone would stop talking about those fish. After all, that happened when I was just five years old. "I'm in second grade now," I told Dad. "I am very responsible."

Dad looked like he was ready to say something else, so I darted in the door real fast. I headed to the back corner of the store where all the cages were. I didn't look at the birds. I went right past the hamsters and gerbils. I stopped in front of the guinea pigs. They were all huddled in a big glass box. I looked for the perfect guinea pig.

Dad stepped up behind me. "That white one looks cute," he said.

I thought the white guinea pig looked too much like cotton.

"How about the brown one?" Dad said.

I didn't say anything. I was too busy eyeing the one that raced across the cage, sending little flakes of cedar chips flying over the brown one. He had patches of brown, tan, black, and white, as if he couldn't decide what color to be. His hair didn't lie flat. It stuck up in crazy angles like the way some of those rock guitarists wear their hair.

The guinea pig skidded to a stop and nibbled on a little tube that was in the cage. He looked straight at me.

"That's the one," I said. "I'll name him Godzilla!"

"Godzilla?" Dad asked. His voice cracked a little.

I nodded. "Godzilla, the guinea pig with an attitude!"

A girl scooped Godzilla out of the glass box and put him in a cardboard box. "Will you need a cage?" she asked.

"I have an old aquarium," I told her. I was glad Dad didn't tell her what happened to the fish. We had to buy cedar chips, food, and a water bottle. I was going to be the best guinea pig owner!

As soon as we were back in the car, I took Godzilla out of the tiny pet store carton. He sniffed my shirt, my hand, then my nose. He made a little churring noise, reminding me of a cat purring. I could tell right then and there that Godzilla and I were going to be best friends.

3

TOO LATE

As soon as I got home I showed Godzilla to everybody. First Mom, then Margaret. Margaret screamed as if Godzilla were trying to bite her nose. I decided it might be fun to teach Godzilla to chase Margaret.

Margaret acted mad and left the house, yelling to Mom that she was going to Charlene's house because Charlene didn't have a little brother who bothered her. I pretended not to hear her.

Next, I wanted to show Godzilla to Cindy. Cindy is my best friend. She's also my neighbor. She's not like some girls in my class. She likes to play soccer, ride bikes, and dig worms. Just like me.

The phone rang before I got out my back door. It was a boy and he asked for Margaret. I wrote down his name and number and put the paper on the shelf next to the phone.

Godzilla liked being held. For a while. Then he got squirmy. I needed something to carry him in. I sat Godzilla on the shelf near the phone and went to get my backpack.

There was nothing in my backpack except homework. I stuffed the papers down to the bottom and went back for Godzilla. Godzilla was busy. Busy chewing paper. The paper with Margaret's phone message! I grabbed the paper.

Too late. Godzilla had eaten the part with the number. I swallowed. Margaret was going to be mad. There was nothing worse than an older sister who was mad. She had ways of making my life miserable. Ways I didn't even want to think about.

I scooped up Godzilla and zipped him into my backpack, leaving it open just a little so Godzilla had plenty of air. After all, I was the most responsible boy in the second grade. I knew an animal needed air to breathe.

I looked to make sure no one was watching. Then I stuffed what was left of Margaret's phone message in my pocket and ran out the back door to introduce Cindy to Godzilla.

4
THE HOMEWORK LAW

Cindy thought Godzilla was great. She liked him better than her ant farm. After all, there wasn't much you could do with pet ants except watch them work.

We played with Godzilla all afternoon and all the next day, too. Godzilla liked it when we made tunnels out of grocery bags.

If he couldn't find his way through them, he just ate a hole in one of the bags.

I hated leaving him in the aquarium on Monday, but Mom said I couldn't take him to school. Godzilla looked sad, but I promised to come home right after school.

School is not my favorite place. It's hard to sit still and listen to Mr. Morris and all his directions.

"Parker?" I heard all of a sudden. "Earth to Parker?" Mr. Morris was looking at me and saying my name over and over. A few kids giggled.

"Yes, Mr. Morris?" I felt my face turning red.

"Do you have your spelling homework?"

"It's in my backpack," I told him. Mom

always made me do my homework as soon as I got home. Then I had to pack it in my backpack. That way Mom said I wouldn't forget it the next day. Mom called it the homework law.

I hurried to the back of the room where we hung our backpacks on a long row of hooks. I pulled out the papers in the bottom. I found an old math paper with Mr. Morris's red C on top. There was a note Cindy wrote me last week. And there was my spelling homework. Well . . . part of it. Actually, only my name and the first three sentences were left.

I swallowed. Hard. Then I turned and faced Mr. Morris. He was waiting. So was everyone in my class. They all looked at me.

I was a very responsible second-grader, so

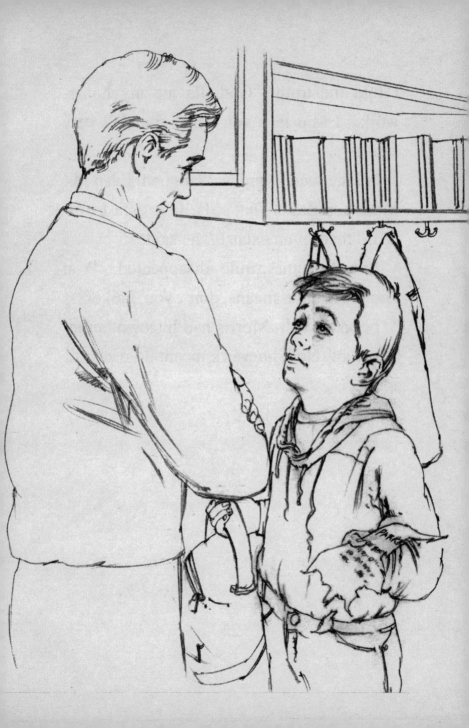

I told the truth. "Godzilla ate my home-work," I said in a voice that sounded very small.

All the second-graders laughed. Even Mr. Morris smiled. "That's the first time I ever heard that for an excuse," he said.

But then the smile disappeared. "You know what that means, don't you, Parker?"

I nodded. Mr. Morris had his own home-work law. No homework meant no recess.

5

A GOOD FRIEND

Cindy walked home with me after school. She told me about the soccer game at recess. "It was a great game," she said. "But it would have been more fun if you were playing."

Cindy was a very good friend.

"Do you want to come over?" she asked.

I shook my head. "I have chores."

My mom said all kids have chores. Cindy didn't have chores. She thought my mom and dad were old-fashioned because they made Margaret and me work. She said making kids work was against the law. I told Mom that and she laughed. I still had to do chores.

As soon as I got home, I took Godzilla from the aquarium. I could tell he was glad to see me because he squealed three times when I walked in my room. He made his little churring noise as soon as I picked him up. His whole body rumbled with happy sounds.

First I did my homework, because I was a very responsible second-grader. Godzilla tried to nibble a corner of my science report, but I didn't let him. When I finished, I was sure to put my report in the bottom of my backpack so I was ready for school.

My first chore was the bathroom. I wiped off the counters. It didn't take very long, but by the time I finished Godzilla had already nibbled a hole in the tissue box. I turned the box around so nobody would see.

I gathered the newspapers to take to the recycling bin in our garage. That was when Margaret came home from school. She let the door slam extra hard.

"Where is that rug rat?" she screamed. "I'm going to kill him."

I gathered Godzilla in my arms, but she

wasn't talking about him. She was yelling about me.

Dad came into the kitchen just in time. Margaret looked like she really meant the part about killing me.

"What's the problem?" he asked.

I had always heard about people seething, but I never knew exactly what it meant. Now I knew. It meant someone got so red in the face and she breathed so hard she looked as if she were ready to explode. Margaret was seething.

She pointed her finger at my nose. "He didn't give me my phone message!" she yelled.

"What phone message?" Dad asked.

I knew she was talking about the phone message Godzilla ate.

Dad looked at me. "Parker," he said, "you know you are to write down the name and number of everybody who calls."

I nodded.

"Then why didn't you?" my sister yelled.

"I did," I said. My voice shook just a little. "But Godzilla . . ."

"Godzilla what?" Margaret hissed.

"He ate it," I told her.

Margaret started to yell again, but Dad held up his hand and Margaret got quiet. "Is anybody bleeding?" he asked Margaret. This is what Dad always asked when he wanted us to know that life was not about to end.

She shook her head. "No."

He asked his second question. "Is anybody dying?"

"No," she huffed.

Dad took a deep breath. "Keep Godzilla away from Margaret's phone messages," he told me. Then he went back to his office where he worked on people's taxes.

I could tell Margaret was still seething. I grabbed the newspapers, sat Godzilla on top of them, and ran out the back door. By the time we got to the garage, Godzilla had already nibbled the weather forecast and he was working on the comics. I took the papers out of his mouth and stuffed them in the recycling bin.

Godzilla and I sneaked in the back door. No sign of Margaret. I only had one more chore. Mail all the envelopes Mom filled with checks to pay our monthly bills. I told

Dad I was going to the mailbox at the corner of our street. Then I was going to Cindy's house. Dad didn't look up from his calculator, but he nodded.

I tossed the envelopes in my backpack and put Godzilla inside. Then I was out the door. I wanted to run to the mailbox, but I didn't want Godzilla to get sick so I walked. I was being very responsible.

I got to the mailbox and pulled out the envelopes. Godzilla was sitting on one. I gently pulled it out from under him. That was when I saw it. One of the envelopes was full of teeth marks. Part of it was missing. The part with the stamp. I knew I couldn't mail it without a stamp, so I put it back in my backpack. Then I mailed the rest.

When I got to her house, Cindy could tell right away I had a problem. Like I said, Cindy is a very good friend. I told her Godzilla ate my homework. I told her he ate Margaret's phone message. I pulled out the envelope. Godzilla had eaten more of it. He had eaten what was inside. I showed her what was left.

"I'm afraid Godzilla will be stewed for dinner if Mom and Dad find out he ate the check inside the envelope," I told Cindy.

"What are you going to do?" Cindy asked. "Are you going to tell them?"

I thought about it. I remembered what Dad always said when he wanted us to know life was not about to end.

"Is anybody bleeding?" I asked Cindy.

She shook her head.

"Is anyone dying?" I asked.

She shook her head again.

I tore what was left of the envelope into tiny pieces. Then I flushed them down the toilet.

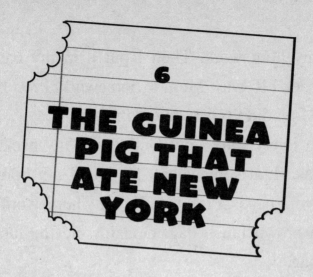

6
THE GUINEA PIG THAT ATE NEW YORK

I had a plan. All I had to do was keep Godzilla away from paper. Then everything would be fine.

Margaret forgot about Godzilla's appetite for phone messages. Nobody found out about the check Godzilla ate. My plan was working. Well, almost.

As soon as I got home from school, I did

my homework. Then I put it in my back-pack. It was Mom's homework law. But Mom didn't plan on Godzilla.

Every time I put Godzilla in my pack to take him somewhere, he found my home-work pages. I tried stuffing my homework in a brown lunch bag. Godzilla ate the lunch bag.

I tried putting my homework in a plastic bag. He ate that, too. I even tried hiding my homework in the little mesh pocket of my backpack. Godzilla chewed right through the material to get to my spelling home-work.

He usually just ate a little corner of my papers. But by the end of the week, I had had to miss recess three times because

Godzilla ate so much I couldn't turn in my homework.

Each day I told Mr. Morris the truth. Godzilla ate it. Each time the class laughed. Mr. Morris shook his head and wrote a grade in his book next to my name. I knew what the grade was: F.

On Saturday, I watched cartoons with Godzilla. Mom sat on the couch looking through cookbooks. She liked to make different recipes. She made a list of all the things she needed to buy at the grocery store. When she finished her list she plopped the cookbooks and list on the table and stood up.

"Don't forget to make your bed," she said. Then she went outside to help Dad clean out the garage. I didn't know where Margaret was. I didn't care.

I kept watching cartoons. I liked it when the house was quiet. Nobody but me and Godzilla.

A commercial interrupted the show. I put Godzilla on the table so he wouldn't hide under the couch or anything. Then I got a bowl of cereal and chocolate milk. I didn't take very long. But it was long enough.

By the time I got back to the family room, Godzilla had Mom's grocery list. I grabbed Godzilla, but he had already eaten most of it.

"You're not supposed to eat paper," I said. But Godzilla churred. He was so happy I was holding him. I couldn't stay mad at him when he did that.

I knew the only way to keep Mom from

getting mad at Godzilla was to be responsible. I turned off the cartoons so I could concentrate. I got a clean piece of paper. Then I made Mom a new grocery list. I didn't know a grocery list could take so long, but finally I was done. I read it over and smiled. Mom would see how responsible I was. I planned meals for every day. Good meals. I stuffed the list in Mom's purse.

Cindy and I had big plans for the day. We were going to build a fort out of cardboard boxes. I packed Godzilla in my backpack and went out the back door.

Building our fort took all afternoon. Godzilla liked our fort almost as much as we did. But we had to watch him or he would eat holes in the walls.

We played Godzilla was the real Godzilla

monster and he was eating all the buildings in New York City. We used Cindy's army men to try to fight him. Godzilla just looked at them and squeaked.

Cindy giggled. "Godzilla," she said, "the guinea pig that ate New York!"

When I finally got home it was almost time for dinner. I came in the back door. Mom was waiting for me. So was Dad. They both looked at me. They were not smiling. Mom waved a piece of paper at me. It was the grocery list I wrote.

"What is this?" Mom asked.

"A grocery list," I told her.

"What happened to the one that took me all morning to make?" she asked.

I hugged Godzilla until he gave a little

squeak. Then I told the truth. "Godzilla ate it."

Mom and Dad glared at Godzilla.

"I did what was responsible," I said. "I made a new list."

Mom looked at the list I had made. She started reading. "Hot dogs? Pizza? Potato chips? Candy bars?" She said each thing like it was a question. She acted as if she was going to read the rest of the list, but then she just took a deep breath. "You and Godzilla are grounded."

I had never been grounded before. I had to spend the rest of the weekend in my room. Godzilla was not allowed out of his aquarium. I knew we were in trouble. Big trouble.

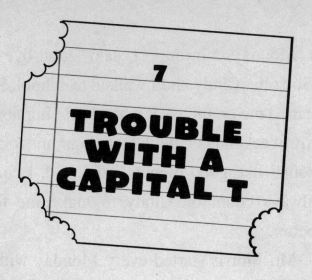

7
TROUBLE WITH A CAPITAL T

There were two good things about being sent to my room. First, Margaret couldn't make fun of me. Second, I could make sure Godzilla didn't eat anything he shouldn't eat.

By Sunday night, Mom wasn't mad anymore. But I was smart. I made sure to keep Godzilla out of sight.

41

Monday morning, I said good-bye to Godzilla. Cindy and I walked to school. She patted me on the back when I told her about my weekend. "I think hot dogs and pizza sound like good dinners," she said. I could always count on Cindy to make me feel better.

Mr. Morris started every Monday with a practice spelling test. I missed most of the words. That meant I had to practice them all week long for the final test on Friday. I wished I could be smart like Cindy. She only missed one word.

Next, we had reading groups. I'm a good reader. This was my favorite part of the day. My reading group was reading a story about a boy who wanted to keep a dog he had found. I knew how the boy felt.

After reading, we had science. Mr. Morris asked us to turn in our reports. I hopped up. Mine was in my pack. I did a great job. I wrote three paragraphs about guinea pigs.

I dug in my pack. Mr. Morris was waiting. So was everyone else. When I pulled out my math homework I got a funny feeling in my stomach. A corner of the paper was nibbled. I finally found my science report. I guess Godzilla was like me. He liked science better than math because Godzilla decided to eat my report instead of the math paper. It was completely ruined.

I swallowed hard and faced Mr. Morris. I showed him the shredded piece of paper. The rest of the class knew what I was going to say. They giggled. Mr. Morris knew what I was going to say. He frowned.

"Godzilla ate it," I said in a tiny voice.

Mr. Morris shook his head. He picked up his grade book and his red grading pen. I knew what he was writing next to my name. Another F.

I sat down, remembering how long it took to write those three paragraphs about guinea pigs. I also remembered I forgot to write something in my report. Keep paper away from guinea pigs.

Cindy patted my shoulder on her way to recess. I didn't bother looking up. Soon, I heard my friends outside. They were playing soccer. I was rewriting my science report.

Mr. Morris waited until I handed him my new report. It was only one paragraph long. He took a deep breath. "You haven't been turning in your homework," he said.

I nodded. I already knew that. I had missed four recesses because I didn't turn in my homework.

"I am worried about your grades," Mr. Morris said.

I didn't know why he was worried. I was the one who missed recess. I was the one who got F's. Not Mr. Morris. I would be the one who had to show the report card to my parents. And in my family, F's meant trouble. Trouble with a capital T.

"I want to help you do better," Mr. Morris said. "From now on, no more stories about Godzilla."

I nodded again. The other second-graders came back in from recess. I walked back to my desk and waited for the rest of the day to pass.

"What are you going to do?" Cindy asked as we walked home. "You can't keep missing recess. We need you on our soccer team."

"I can't keep missing homework," I added. "I'll have all F's on my report card."

Cindy's eyes got big. "Your parents will kill you."

"No," I said in my most serious voice. "They'll kill Godzilla!"

8

SAVED BY THE BELL

I couldn't let Godzilla eat any more homework. I was very careful. I didn't put Godzilla in my backpack until I took out my homework. I put my papers in a safe place on my toy shelf where Godzilla couldn't get them. Every morning, I put my homework back in my pack. I was being very responsible. Things were going great. My plan was working. Until Thursday. That's the day I forgot to put my homework back in my backpack before I left for school.

When Mr. Morris asked for my math, I didn't tell him Godzilla ate it. I told the truth. "I left it at home."

I could tell Mr. Morris was not happy. He closed his eyes and counted to five.

I missed recess again.

It was my turn to wash the dishes that night. Margaret got to watch television. Mom helped me dry the dishes and put them away. That was what we were doing when Margaret stomped into the kitchen. "The cable is not working," she said. "Now I can't watch my favorite show."

Mom looked up a number in the phone book, picked up the phone, and punched in the numbers. She told someone about our cable. Then she was quiet for a while. "Are you sure?" she finally asked. "I see," she said. "I'll have it to you tomorrow."

Mom hung up the phone. "They didn't get this month's check in the mail," she said.

"How could you forget to pay the cable bill?" Margaret moaned. "It's the most important one!"

"I wrote the check," Mom said. "And Parker mailed it last week."

They were looking at me. I swallowed hard.

"You DID mail that stack of envelopes, didn't you?" Mom asked.

I nodded. It was not a lie. I did mail a stack of envelopes.

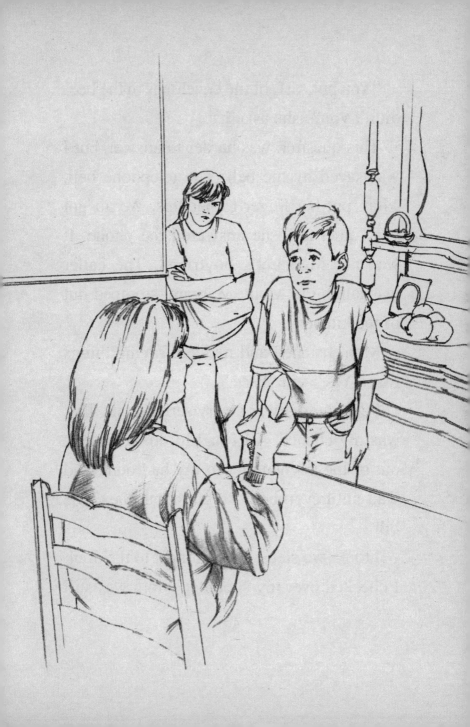

"You put ALL of the envelopes in the box, didn't you?" she asked.

This question was harder to answer, but I was saved by the bell. The telephone bell. Mom put her finger to her lips. We all got very quiet and she answered the phone. It was not Margaret's boyfriend. The caller was talking to Mom. Margaret stomped out of the kitchen.

Mom listened and nodded, saying things like, "Yes," and "I see."

I could tell it was a very serious call. This was my chance. All I had to do was sneak out of the kitchen, get to my bedroom, and wait until everybody forgot about the cable bill.

I took two steps. I was almost to the door. I checked over my shoulder. Mom was still listening to the voice on the phone. She didn't look happy. I took another step.

Just then a shadow fell across the kitchen. Dad was standing in front of the door, blocking my way. In one hand was a gobbled-up piece of green paper. I looked closer. It was money and it had a big number on it.

In his other hand was Godzilla.

9

BIG TROUBLE

Margaret stood behind Dad. They all waited until Mom hung up the phone.

Nobody said anything. Except Godzilla. He squeaked. I think Dad was holding him too tight but I knew better than to tell him.

"Your pet ate a one-hundred-dollar bill," Dad said.

When I used Dad's calculator the day before, I let Godzilla explore on Dad's desk. I should have left him in my room instead.

I wanted to remind Dad that no one was bleeding or dying, but one hundred dollars was a lot of money. I kept my mouth shut.

"That's not all he ate, is it?" Mom asked.

I shook my head. "No."

"That was Mr. Morris on the phone," Mom told Dad. "He thought Parker was making up stories about why he didn't have his homework."

"Why haven't you been turning in your homework?" Dad asked.

I took a deep breath. "Godzilla ate it."

"And Parker didn't mail all the envelopes," Mom added. "The company shut off our cable service."

"Why didn't you mail the envelope?" Dad asked, but he already knew the answer.

I told the truth. "Godzilla ate it."

"GODZILLA!" Margaret screamed. "I'm going to kill that rat and roast it on the charcoal grill."

"He's not a rat," I told her. Margaret wasn't interested in learning about guinea pigs. Instead, she grabbed for Godzilla.

"NO!" I screamed. "Don't hurt him."

Dad lifted Godzilla high in the air. Godzilla squeaked. Godzilla was in big trouble!

I had to think fast to save Godzilla. "It's

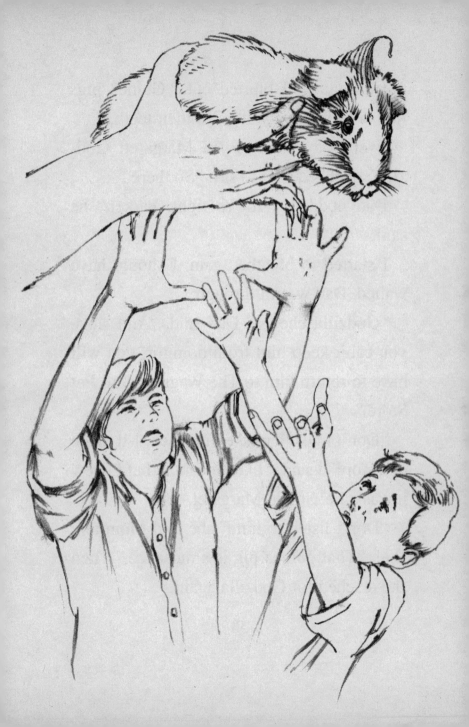

not his fault," I blurted out. "Guinea pigs like to chew things. It helps their teeth."

Everybody froze. Even Margaret. Godzilla squeaked as if to say, "So there."

Dad nodded. "You're right, Parker," he said.

I started to breathe again. I should have waited. Dad wasn't through.

"Godzilla chews," Dad said. "And since you can't keep him from doing it, you will have to return him to The Wagging Tail Pet Store."

"Don't make me take him back. I'll make him stop!" I said it like I meant it, but I knew it was a lie. So did Margaret.

"Don't listen to him," she told Mom and Dad. "That guinea pig is a nuisance." Then she reached for Godzilla again.

I ran across the room and tackled Margaret around the ankles. Dad jumped back and stumbled on a kitchen chair. Mom tried to keep Dad from falling. Godzilla squeaked.

That was when the phone rang. I grabbed for the phone. I hoped it was the police so I could tell them to come right away and save Godzilla.

It wasn't the police. It was Mr. Morris. He had a plan.

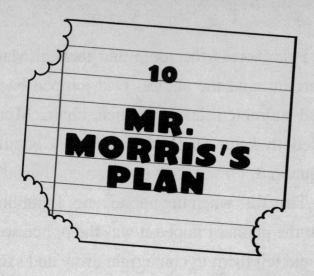

10

MR. MORRIS'S PLAN

Mr. Morris looked up from the papers he was grading. "You're early," he said.

But he knew I would be. Now I always get to school early. Mr. Morris handed me my math paper from the day before. There were a lot of red marks on it. Math is not my favorite subject.

"Maybe your sister can help you with

math," Mr. Morris said. He obviously didn't know Margaret.

I headed for the back of the room. That was where Mr. Morris had put the big glass aquarium. I lifted the top and reached inside.

Godzilla squeaked. Then he made his churring noise. His whole body rumbled with happy noises. I knew he was glad to see me. I was glad to see him, too.

The rest of the second-graders came into our room. Cindy came back to pet Godzilla before putting her lunch away.

Sharing Godzilla with the rest of the second grade wasn't the best part about Mr. Morris's plan, but it was better than what Margaret had in mind. She wanted to cook Godzilla for dinner. I didn't like Mom and Dad's idea of taking Godzilla back to The

Wagging Tail Pet Store, either. So when Mr. Morris said Godzilla could be a class pet, I decided it was the best idea of all. I did the responsible thing. Now Godzilla lives in Mr. Morris's classroom.

There are some good things about having Godzilla as a class pet. For one thing, I don't mind school as much. Mr. Morris even lets me take Godzilla to my desk when I finish all my work.

Ever since I brought Godzilla to the classroom, the rest of the second-graders have been very nice to me. That's because Mr. Morris said I was in charge of deciding who gets to play with Godzilla.

Godzilla and I also have a special understanding. Sometimes I give him treats to nibble. Like today.

I looked at the math paper Mr. Morris gave me. The one with all the red marks. Then I checked to make sure Mr. Morris wasn't looking.

I smiled and gave Godzilla his special snack.

The more things change...the more confused Amber Brown gets!

FOREVER AMBER BROWN

by Paula Danziger

Amber Brown has already gone through a
lot of changes — but now Max, her mother's
boyfriend, is asking her mom to marry him!
Why can't things just stay the same *forever*?

Coming in August to bookstores everywhere.

Have you read Amber's other adventures?
AMBER BROWN IS NOT A CRAYON
YOU CAN'T EAT YOUR CHICKEN POX, AMBER BROWN
AMBER BROWN GOES FOURTH
AMBER BROWN WANTS EXTRA CREDIT